Created By
JIM DAVIS

Written by Michael Teitelbaum
Designed and Illustrated
by Mike Fentz

SCHOLASTIC INC.
New York Toronto London Auckland Sydney
Mexico City New Delhi Hong Kong Buenos Aires

ISBN 0-439-70543-6



12 11 10 9 8 7 6 5 4 3 2 1 4 5 6 7 8 9 10

Printed in the U.S.A.
First printing, November 2004

“It’s Christmas Eve!” said Jon Arbuckle. He had just finished putting a star atop his Christmas tree. “Come on, Garfield, Odie. We’re going downtown to see Santa!”

Garfield was curled up in a corner. “I thought Santa delivered,” he said with a yawn. “Like the pizza guy.”

Odie came bounding into the room, panting and drooling. This was his way of telling Jon he was ready to go.

Garfield stumbled to the window and cleared a small circle in the frost with his paw. He saw snow gently falling.

"There's white stuff falling from the sky," Garfield muttered. "And it's not sugar. Maybe I'll just hibernate for three more months!"

"I'm taking the two of you downtown to Sweeney's Department Store to see Santa," Jon said, pulling his reindeer sweater over his head. "You can tell him what you want for Christmas!"

"What I want is to stay home and take a nap," Garfield groaned.

"I always loved going to see Santa when I was a kid," Jon continued, slipping on his scarf, heavy winter coat, and hat. He finished by zipping up his hood and pulling on his gloves. "Come on, Garfield. Now!"

By the time Jon finished getting dressed, he could barely move.

Garfield rolled his eyes, following Jon out the door. "He's only going to the car!"

Garfield said. "You'd think he was going to the North Pole or something!"

Odie scooted out the door. Slipping on the snow, he slid down the walk, spun around three times, and then crashed into the car.

"Show-off," Garfield mumbled. Then he climbed into the backseat beside Odie.

A short time later, Jon, Garfield, and Odie arrived at Sweeney's Department Store. Decorated Christmas trees lined the area where Santa sat on a big wooden chair.

Whining children stood in a long line, waiting to see Santa. Garfield and Odie joined the back of the line. Jon, still all bundled up, beamed with pride.

"Just tell Santa what you want," Jon told Garfield.

"What I want," Garfield muttered, "is to not be seen with you. You look like you're ready to walk on Mars. Which, come to think of it, doesn't sound like a bad idea."

The line inched along. Following a long, boring wait, Garfield and Odie finally reached Santa. One of Santa's helpers lifted Garfield and placed him onto the big man's lap.

"Nice belly," Garfield mumbled. "Not

as nice as mine, of course, but then I work hard at maintaining my shape."

"Well, my little friend," Santa began. "What do you want for Christmas?"

"A bathtub-sized lasagna, and—"

Garfield was interrupted by the sudden appearance of an elf. The little man, with a red beard, green hat, and green pointy shoes, hurried to Santa's side.

"Nice outfit, pal," Garfield quipped. "Are they holding auditions for *Peter Pan*?"

The elf leaned close to Santa and whispered into his ear. Santa's face turned pale.

"What's the matter?" Garfield asked, noticing Santa's frightened expression. "Does the rental company need their costume back early?"

Santa looked out at the endless line of children. He sighed, then whispered back to the elf. The elf nodded, then turned to Garfield.

"You've got to help us," the elf said to Garfield, who looked over his shoulder.

"You talking to me?" Garfield asked. "Because I heard the word *help*, which usually means action, and action involves movement, and that's where you lose me."

"I am Wumbly, an elf from the North Pole," the elf explained.

"Right, I get it," Garfield replied. "You look good in the costume, too."

"No, you don't understand," Wumbly said. "I'm a *real* elf. I've come here because there's a problem with Santa."

"I don't know," Garfield said. "He looks okay to me."

"Not him," Wumbly said. "The *real* Santa!"

"The real Santa?" Garfield asked.

"Yes," Wumbly replied. "Department-store Santas are chosen by the real Santa to be his helpers. The real Santa is too busy preparing for Christmas. I've asked this helper Santa to come with me. He wants to, but can't bear to disappoint all these children."

"Hey!" shouted a man in the line, holding a crying child. "Give someone else a chance, will you!"

"Please come with me," Wumbly begged Garfield. "You've got to help!"

"I don't think so," Garfield replied, not really believing the elf.

"You know, I have some pull with the real Santa," Wumbly said. "If you help, I might just be able to arrange that bathtub-sized lasagna."

"Now you're talking!" Garfield said, climbing down from Santa's lap.

With Odie hot on his heels, Garfield followed Wumbly into a small room behind Santa's chair. In the room, Garfield spied boxes of ornaments, extra elf costumes, and a giant candy cane.

Wumbly picked up a huge cloth sack, like the one Santa used to carry his presents. When he opened the sack, a strange golden glow poured out.

"Looks like someone left the light on in Santa's sack," Garfield said.

"Please," Wumbly pleaded. "Just step into the sack. We have no time to lose!"

"You want me to step into a bag?" Garfield asked. "It's not even a bag of chips!"

"Please," Wumbly begged again.

"Do it for Santa."

"Well," Garfield moaned.

"Then do it for the bathtub-sized lasagna," Wumbly said, flashing a smile.

"Done!" Garfield said. He and Odie stepped into the bag and vanished.

Jon watched as Garfield and Odie went with the elf into the room behind Santa's chair. *Wow!* he thought. *They're going with that elf. He must have some special treat for them. Hmmm . . . this might be a good time to finish my last-minute shopping. I'm sure Garfield and Odie will be fine for a little while.*

Jon unzipped his coat, lifted his sweater, and reached into his shirt pocket. *Rats!* he thought. *I left my shopping list at home. But I should have enough time to drive home and get it. Those guys won't even miss me!*

As Jon drove home, the snow grew thicker. By the time he pulled into his driveway, the snow was coming down heavily. The wind whipped the snow into blinding drifts.

Worried, Jon turned on his TV.

"This is a special weather bulletin," the announcer reported. "An unexpected blizzard has struck the entire area and is expected to last all night. Please do not attempt to drive unless it's an absolute emergency!"

"Oh, no!" Jon cried. "Now I can't get back to the store. I'll have to wait for this to blow over. Gee, I hope Garfield and Odie are okay!"

Garfield and Odie were surrounded by blinding white light. When the light faded, they found themselves in a large

room. Everywhere he looked, Garfield saw elves hard at work. Some were building toys. Others were wrapping boxes with colorful Christmas paper.

A large conveyor belt snaked through the room, carrying wrapped presents. At the end of the conveyor, elves placed the boxes onto a big sleigh parked just outside.

"Welcome to the North Pole," Wumbly said. "This is Santa's workshop."

"The North Pole!" Garfield ex-

claimed. "But how did we get here?"

"Elf magic," Wumbly replied.

Garfield hurried to a nearby window. Looking out, he saw a winter wonderland. Snow fell gently, clinging to the branches of tall pine trees. Rolling white hills stretched as far as the eye could see.

"Well, it's sure not Jon's backyard,"

Garfield said. "I don't see any plastic flamingos."

Odie trotted over to a giant candy cane and began licking it.

"Uh, Odie, that's a prop," Wumbly said. "It's just there to add some extra cheer to the workshop."

Odie nodded happily at Wumbly. Then he continued licking the giant painted candy cane.

Another elf came rushing up to Garfield and Wumbly. He had a long white

beard, a pointy green hat, and pointy green shoes.

"Thank goodness you brought help, Wumbly!" the elf cried.

"This is Nimgal," Wumbly said, pointing to the other elf. "He is Santa's chief elf and second-in-command. Wumbly, this is Garfield and . . ."

Wumbly turned to Odie. Odie looked back at him, wagging his tongue, which was now covered in red paint. ". . . and that's Odie," Wumbly finished.

"Something terrible has happened," Nimgal said.

"I know," Garfield said. "I'm late for my afternoon nap!"

"Someone kidnapped Santa!" Nimgal explained. "An elf named Alfip, the head toy maker, wanted more power. He was tired of making toys all year while Santa got all the glory. And so he kidnapped Santa and took him into the snowy wastelands of the North Pole."

"Wow!" Garfield replied, looking out the window again. "Snowy wastelands. That covers a lot of ground. But then again, so do I."

"I can't rescue Santa by myself," Nimgal went on. "And all the other elves are busy preparing for Christmas. When Wumbly heard the news, he went to get help. To be honest, I was hoping for more experienced helpers. Perhaps even a bloodhound with a sharp nose."

"Odie is a dumb hound with a red tongue," Garfield pointed out. "Does that count?" Odie's entire face was now covered in red paint from the wooden candy cane.

"Make that a red *face*," Garfield corrected himself.

"It's Christmas Eve, and we have less than a day to find Santa!" Nimgal said anxiously. "Will you and Odie help?"

"I don't know," Garfield balked. "I'm more comfortable dealing with waist*lines* than waste*lands*. Besides, the thought of trudging through the snow just leaves me cold."

"But the children of the world will be so disappointed if there is no Christmas," Nimgal pointed out.

"Well, I'm not sure," Garfield said as Odie trotted up beside him. Wumbly took a cloth and wiped the red paint from Odie's face.

"And think of poor Santa, freezing out there!" Nimgal added.

"Well, that snow out there, it's awfully . . . snowy," Garfield whined.

Glancing at Garfield's belly, Nimgal tried a new approach. "Santa's got the key to the North Pole's secret candy closet."

"What are we waiting for?" Garfield exclaimed.

After outfitting Garfield and Odie with parkas and backpacks filled with camping supplies, Nimgal grabbed his high-powered flashlight.

"Are you sure we brought enough food?" Garfield asked, struggling under the weight of his pack.

"We each have enough for four days," Nimgal explained.

"Well, that should take care of me for the next few hours," Garfield said. "But what are you and Odie going to eat?"

"Good luck," Wumbly said as Nimgal, Garfield, and Odie headed to the door.

"GOOD LUCK!" cried all the elves in the workshop.

"Please find Santa," Wumbly said, choking back tears. "Christmas depends on your bravery."

"Great," replied Garfield. "Maybe you guys should start planning for Valentine's Day."

Then Garfield followed Odie and Nimgal out into the snow.

The three searchers set off on their quest. Nimgal took the lead. Garfield followed, complaining as he walked. Odie brought up the rear. Soon the snow got deeper and walking became more difficult.

"Do we have a destination," Garfield asked, "or do you just enjoy strolling through deep snow?"

"There's an old abandoned cave at the top of an ice mountain on the other side of a lake, just a short hike from here," Nimgal explained. "It's a perfect place to hide somebody. Alfip might be holding Santa in that cave. It's a good place to start, in any case."

"No, appetizers are a good place to start," Garfield said. "Followed by soup, salad, main course, and dessert."

"We've got cucumber sandwiches and protein bars in our backpacks," Nimgal offered.

"Oh, great. Health food," Garfield replied. "Still, food is food. Let's eat!"

"Garfield! We just began!" exclaimed Nimgal. "If we eat all our food now, what will we do later?"

"Watch TV, then take a nap?" Garfield said hopefully.

"We're on a rescue mission," Nimgal

reminded him. "Remember?"

"Hey, I have an idea," Garfield said as he struggled to take another step. "Why don't you just zap us to the mountaintop and save a lot of effort? If there's one thing I hate, it's effort! Well, that and dieting."

"I can't. My elf magic grows weaker the farther I get from the workshop," Nimgal explained. "And we need to save my magic to help us cross the lake. I'm afraid

we have to get through this snow the old-fashioned way."

"What's that?" Garfield asked. "Pay someone to carry us?"

As the trio continued, the snow got even deeper and Garfield got even crankier. "You didn't bring a periscope by any chance, did you?" Garfield asked as the snow approached his chin.

Suddenly Garfield turned around. There was no sign of Odie. "Odie's gone!" he cried. "And he was carrying some of the food!"

Odie's ears popped out of the snow just behind Garfield. Then he gulped down a mouthful of snow, took one step forward, and sank into the whiteness again.

"Perhaps you're right, Garfield," Nimgal said. "At this rate, we'll never find Santa in time. I suppose a little magic couldn't hurt. I hope."

Nimgal pressed together his fingers, closed his eyes, and concentrated. Red waves of energy poured from his hands. The red magic glowed for a few moments, then vanished. Along the area where the red energy had been, the snow magically melted, forming a path that stretched out before them.

"Nice trick," Garfield said in amazement. "Do you also do driveways?"

"We've no time to waste," Nimgal said. "The lake is just ahead."

With a clear path ahead, Nimgal, Garfield, and Odie picked up their pace. A few minutes later, they arrived at the shore of a huge lake.

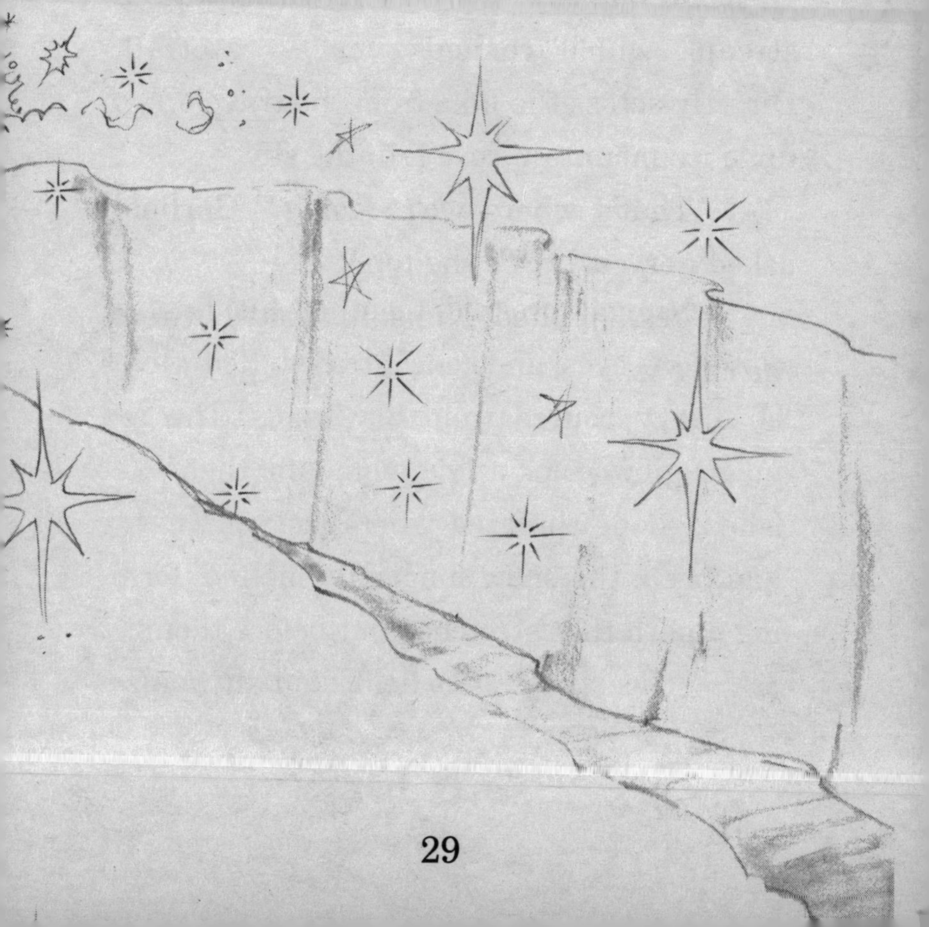

The cold water on the lake's surface glistened like diamonds. Snow lined the shore, and enormous chunks of ice floated in the lake. All around the shore, polar bears frolicked, diving into the lake to catch fish, then climbing back out and rolling around in the snow.

On one side the lake narrowed into a stream, which rushed over a waterfall. Directly across the lake from the travelers, a huge ice mountain rose into the sky.

"That's where we're going?" Garfield asked nervously. "To the top?"

"Yes," replied Nimgal. "That's where the cave is."

"I wish I had hidden in bed," Garfield said. "How are we going to cross this lake? I don't see any boats."

"As I told you," Nimgal said. "Elf magic. I will create an ice bridge across the lake. Follow me."

“As I recall, that’s how we got into this mess!” Garfield whined.

Nimgal led Garfield and Odie out to the edge of a narrow peninsula. The elf once again brought his fingertips together, closed his eyes, and concentrated.

A dull white glow radiated from his hands, stretching a few yards out into the lake. He scrunched his face up, concentrating even harder. A few seconds later, the white glow faded.

Nimgal sighed. “Not enough magic left,” he said sadly. “I must have used too much to clear the snow. And now we’re farther from the workshop. My magic is just too weak.”

“Well, we gave it a good try,” Garfield said, turning around to leave.

*CA-RACK!*

A loud cracking sound filled the air as their tip of the peninsula broke away. Nimgal, Garfield, and Odie floated out toward the middle of the lake on a small chunk of ice.

"There must have been too much weight on the tip of the peninsula!" Nimgal shouted.

Nimgal and Odie both turned and stared at Garfield.

"What?!" he shouted. "Why are you looking at me? I ate only three lasagnas last night. How was I supposed to know that this overgrown ice cube had a two-lasagna weight limit? Besides, can't we just float across the lake?"

Nimgal shook his head. "The current is pulling us to the side," he said. "It's bringing us right toward the waterfall!"

Garfield and Odie stared in horror. Water and ice floes poured over the falls, plunging one hundred feet to a river below.

"This might be a good time to eat those sandwiches and protein bars," Garfield said. "Because I don't think we'll be around to eat them later!"

The ice chunk raced toward the waterfall.

Nimgal pressed his fingers together, desperately trying to whip up some magic. Nothing happened.

They were now just a few yards from the waterfall. "Well, Odie," Garfield began. "This is it. The end. You know, there's something I always wanted to tell you."

Odie looked up at Garfield. Small tears formed in the corners of his eyes.

"I just want to tell you that it was me who put the rubber chicken into your bowl at

Thanksgiving. And it was me who put the plastic wrap over your water bowl. You licked that thing for three days. And it was also me who—"

Suddenly the ice chunk slowed down, then began moving away from the waterfall's edge.

"Your magic worked!" Garfield shouted. "You did it!"

"No," Nimgal replied, pointing to the water. "It wasn't me. It was them!"

Garfield spotted two polar bears swimming furiously. They pushed the ice chunk with their noses as their powerful legs propelled them back toward the middle of the lake.

"Thank you, friends!" Nimgal cried when they were clear of the current.

"Happy to help," replied the polar bear on the left as they continued pushing the ice. "We saw the tip of the peninsula break off and realized that you were in trouble. Someone in your group must have been over the weight limit."

Again, Nimgal and Odie turned to Garfield.

"What!" he cried. "I'm average weight for a cat my height. Well, maybe for three cats my height standing side by side."

"My friends, do you think you could do us another big favor?" Nimgal asked.

"Sure," replied the polar bear on the right. "We've got a pretty light schedule today. Right, Ralph?"

"Let's see, Fred," began the polar bear on the left. "We've got to catch some fish."

"Done," Fred replied.

"Then we've got to roll around in the snow for a while," Ralph added.

"Done."

"And later on, we're going to, let's see. Oh, yeah. Catch some more fish," Ralph finished.

"Looks like we can help," Fred concluded. "What can we do for you?"

"Could you push us to the far side of the lake?" Nimgal asked, pointing toward the mountain. "You see, someone has kidnapped Santa. We're trying to rescue him before the sun goes down and he has to leave on his Christmas Eve journey."

A few minutes later, they reached the far shore. The polar bears shoved the ice chunk up onto the snow. As Nimgal, Garfield, and Odie hopped off, the sky darkened and snow began to fall again.

"Thanks for all your help!" Nimgal said, adjusting his backpack and starting off toward the base of the mountain.

“Anytime,” Fred replied. “And good luck. Santa’s a swell guy. I hope he’s okay.” Then the two polar bears dove back into the lake with a tremendous splash.

“Hey!” Garfield cried, quickly turning his backpack away to avoid the freezing water. “There are sandwiches here!”

Soon the intrepid trio were trudging up the steep side of the snowy mountain. The weather grew worse as a storm moved in.

"Couldn't I just wait back in the workshop until they build an escalator?" Garfield asked.

"Hurry," Nimgal replied. "We don't have much time."

As Odie tramped his way up the mountain, he stuck out his tongue. He loved to catch snowflakes on his tongue. However, he often forgot to pull his tongue back in after the flakes landed. Snow piled up on his tongue until it got so heavy that his head hit the ground, sinking into the snow.

"His head is buried in the snow!" Nimgal cried.

"Oh, that's okay!" Garfield replied. "He doesn't use it anyway."

"Garfield!" Nimgal shouted. "Some help, please!"

"Sheesh!" Garfield exclaimed. "I have to do everything around here!"

Garfield and Nimgal grabbed Odie by his back legs and yanked hard. Odie popped free of the snow and tumbled onto his two rescuers.

Regrouping, the three continued their climb. After what seemed like days to Garfield, but in reality was just a couple of hours, they finally reached the top.

"There it is," Nimgal said, pointing to a dark cave just ahead. "I hope they're inside."

Nimgal pulled out his flashlight and clicked it on. Then he walked into the cave.

"I hope they have a snack bar and a space heater," Garfield said as he and Odie followed the elf.

Inside the cave, Nimgal trained his bright beam onto the icy walls. As the trio moved deeper into the cave, the passageway grew narrower. "If the real Santa looks anything like that guy in the department store, there's no way he'd fit through here," Garfield pointed out.

"Let's go a little farther," Nimgal suggested. "These caves go way back."

The slender passageway soon opened into a large cavern with a high ceiling. Garfield heard a low rumbling. "Either Santa has a bad case of indigestion or someone else is in this cave!" he cried.

Nimgal swung his flashlight toward the noise. There in the light stood an enormous abominable snowman!

"*ROOAAARR!*" the terrifying monster bellowed, revealing his huge teeth.

"It's a yeti!" cried Nimgal, turning and dashing back down the passageway.

"I don't care what his name is," Garfield yelled, close on Nimgal's heels. "I make it a point to never hang around with anyone whose teeth are bigger than I am!"

When they had almost reached the mouth of the cave, Garfield looked back. Odie was nowhere in sight.

"Nimgal, wait!" Garfield cried. "That beast got Odie!" When Garfield turned back around, Nimgal had vanished. Now the cave was silent.

And Garfield was totally alone.

"If I lose track of Nimgal, we'll never find Santa—or our way home," Garfield said to himself. "But someone has to save Odie. ANY VOLUNTEERS . . . volunteers . . . volunteers . . . ?" His voice echoed down the empty corridor.

"I take that as a no," said the flabby tabby.

Garfield moved slowly along the narrow passageway, back toward the cavern. Without Nimgal's flashlight, the corridor got darker as Garfield moved farther from the entrance. Feeling his way along the smooth cold wall, he soon found himself by the cavern. Peering in, he saw a soft light flickering on the far wall.

"Either that yeti just installed mood lighting or he's got a fire going!" Garfield muttered softly. "I only hope that roasted Odie isn't on today's menu!"

Following the curved wall around the cavern, Garfield came to a small archway. *The light is coming from the other side of that archway,* he thought. *I hope I'm not too late. I don't know what I'd do if anything happened to Odie. Well, first I'd eat, but then I'd be very, very upset!*

Garfield heard a strange noise coming through the archway.

*WHISH! TINK! Pad-pad-pad. WHISH! TINK! Pad-pad-pad.*

Bracing for the worst, Garfield stepped through the arch. He found himself in a small room. In the center, a roar-

ing campfire blazed, sending light dancing along the ceiling. A metal cauldron hung above the fire. Garfield heard liquid bubbling in the pot.

"Oh, no!" he cried. "It's Odie stew!"

"Actually," said a voice from the shadows, "it's hot chocolate. Would you like some?"

The yeti stepped from the shadows and offered Garfield a steaming cup of hot chocolate.

Garfield took the cup but eyed the creature suspiciously. "Where's Odie?"

At that moment Odie came trotting over, carrying an icicle in his mouth. He placed the icicle in front of the yeti.

The creature slid the icicle along the slippery floor.

*WHISH!*

Odie dashed after it, grabbing the icicle in his teeth.

*TINK!*

Then Odie came trotting back to the yeti to repeat the game.

*Pad-pad-pad.*

"You've been playing *fetch*?" Garfield asked.

"Yes," the yeti replied. "He's quite good at it."

"So you're not a horrible monster who wants to eat us?" asked Garfield.

"Actually, I'm a vegetarian," the yeti explained. "I have a freezer full of veggies and tofu burgers."

"What, no lasagna?" Garfield asked. "No frozen pizza? You really *are* a monster. Speaking of which, why the big roar when we first came into the cave?"

"I'm not used to visitors," the yeti explained. "You guys startled me, so I roared. You and the elf ran, but Odie came to say hi, and we started this lovely game of fetch. I always wanted a dog, and Odie seems like a great dog."

"There are two words that don't belong together," Garfield mumbled. "*Great* and *dog*."

"So why are you in my cave anyway?" the yeti asked.

Garfield quickly filled in the yeti on their quest to find Santa.

"Santa missing? No Christmas? That's terrible!" said the yeti, sliding the icicle back across the floor. Odie happily ran it down.

"I'll help you guys look for Santa and find your friend."

The yeti grabbed a flaming log from the fire to use as a torch and led Garfield and Odie out of the cave.

"I hope nothing bad happened to Nimgal," Garfield said. "He had a whole backpack full of food! Where could he have gone?"

With the yeti leading the way, Garfield and Odie started down another side of the mountain. Halfway down, Odie watched as a big snowflake landed on his nose. The snowflake tickled, the tickle grew into an itch, and the itch turned into a full-blown sneeze.

*HAH-CHOOO!*

A low, deep rumble sounded from above.

"Uh-oh!" cried the yeti. "Avalanche!"

A huge wave of snow came rushing down the mountain, headed right for the trio!

"Quick!" shouted the yeti. "Get onto my back!"

"That involves climbing," said Garfield. "I was looking forward to going downhill for a change!"

"Now!" shouted the yeti.

Garfield and Odie scrambled onto the yeti's back.

"Hold tight!" he shouted, just as the edge of the wall of snow hit.

Diving forward, the yeti caught the hurtling snow like a surfer catching an ocean wave. Stroking like a swimmer with his powerful arms, the yeti rode the avalanche on his belly.

"Is there a beverage service on this flight?" Garfield asked, hanging onto the yeti's neck for dear life. "Or maybe a little bag of peanuts?"

When they finally came to rest at the bottom of the mountain, Garfield's head was spinning and his eyes were rolling in their sockets. "I need to lie down," he said, trying to stand up straight. "For about six or seven months."

Odie, on the other hand, ran back up a few steps and barked happily at the yeti.

"No, Odie," the yeti said, brushing the snow from his fur. "We can't do that again. We've got to find Santa."

The sky darkened slowly as evening came on. By this time, Garfield was tired, frozen, and almost out of food. As if all that wasn't enough to make him cranky, he now not only had to rescue Santa but had to locate Nimgal as well.

"I'm cold," Garfield whined. "I'm hungry. I'm—"

*Ahoooo!* An eerie howl echoed in the distance.

"I'm sorry," Garfield said. "Was that my stomach growling?"

*AHOOOO!*

The howling grew louder.

"White wolves!" the yeti cried. "I'd know that howl anywhere!"

"White wolves," Garfield repeated. "That doesn't sound good."

*AHOOHOOHOO!*

A chorus of howls came from the opposite direction.

"It's not, especially when there's a whole pack of them," the yeti explained.

"Are they possibly vegetarians?" Garfield asked as the howling grew louder.

"We've got to hide," said the yeti. "But first we've got to find a way to lead them away from us."

"Wait a minute!" Garfield cried. "Can't you frighten them away with your scary yeti roar? You know, *ROOAAARR!*" Garfield raised his arms over his head, imitating the yeti.

Almost in response, the howling increased.

*AHOOHOOHOOHOO!*

"Not when there are this many!" the

yeti replied. "Is there any food left?"

"There's one more sandwich," Garfield reported. Then he eyed the yeti suspiciously.

"Why?"

"Give me the sandwich!" the yeti demanded.

"But it's the last one!" Garfield whined.

"Which would you rather give up?" the yeti asked. "Your sandwich or your life?"

Garfield stared blankly at the yeti.

"Well?" the yeti said.

"I'm thinking!" said Garfield.

"Garfield!"

"All right! All right!" Garfield reluctantly handed over the final cucumber sandwich.

The yeti tore the sandwich into ten tiny pieces. He set the pieces in the snow, a few feet apart, forming a trail leading into a grove of pine trees. Then he bent over and began digging a hole, shoveling snow back through his legs.

"Odie, help me with this!" the yeti shouted as he continued digging.

Odie scampered to the far side of the hole. Facing in the same direction as the yeti, Odie began digging furiously with his paws. A steady stream of snow flew back through his legs—right into the yeti's hole.

"Uh, Odie," the yeti said. "Turn around."

Odie spun around, jumped into the

hole, and began to empty out all the snow he had just tossed in.

*AHOOOOOHOOOOOHOOOOO!*

"They're close!" the yeti exclaimed. "Quick, into the hole."

"There's still time to mush the pieces of the sandwich back together!" Garfield suggested.

"NOW!" the yeti yelled.

"Okay! Okay!" Garfield grumbled. "Sheesh! What a grouchy yeti!"

Garfield, Odie, and the yeti scrunched down into the hole. The yeti reached back out and covered the trio with snow. "There should be enough air in here to last a few minutes," the yeti said. "All we can do now is wait quietly and hope for the best."

From his hiding place, Garfield heard the wolves approach. Their creepy howling was replaced by the sounds of the entire pack sniffing, trying to pick up a scent.

One wolf discovered a small piece of the sandwich and growled a signal to the rest of the pack. One by one the wolves followed the line of sandwich bits into the pine grove. Within a few minutes, they had all gone.

Pushing the snow away, the yeti poked his head out of the hole. "Come on," he said. "Be quick and be quiet, or they'll be back."

"Are those my only choices?" Garfield asked, brushing the snow from his eyes.

The yeti led the two pets away from the pine trees.

Night was falling quickly now, and it became harder to figure out which direction to take.

"I give up!" Garfield announced. "We've risked life and limb, not to mention a sandwich. But it's almost dark, and I don't know how we're going to find our way home, much less rescue anybody."

The yeti sighed deeply. "I'm sorry I couldn't help more, Garfield," he said. "But I've got to return to my cave before it's too dark to find my own way home. You and Odie are welcome to come with me to take shelter for the night."

"Climbing that mountain and facing an avalanche is enough for one day," Garfield said. "We've got to find Nimgal and then get back to Santa's workshop."

"Good luck," said the yeti, shaking Garfield's hand. "You've been a good friend." Then the yeti headed for home.

Garfield looked around and noticed that Odie was nowhere to be seen. "Now where did he go?"

Just as Garfield prepared to set off on yet another search, Odie came trotting up to him, carrying something in his mouth.

"Did you find another icicle?" Garfield asked. "Well, you're too late. Yeti's already on his way home." Then Garfield looked closely at the object in Odie's mouth.

"Nimgal's flashlight!" Garfield exclaimed. "Where did you find it?"

Odie turned and dashed a short distance away. Garfield struggled to keep up but soon arrived at the spot where Odie had picked up the flashlight. Reaching over, Garfield clicked on the light. Its powerful beam revealed a set of footprints.

"Footprints!" Garfield exclaimed. "Small, pointy footprints! It has got to be Nimgal!"

Garfield and Odie picked up Nimgal's trail. The duo followed the footprints by the light of the flashlight, which Odie clutched tightly in his mouth as if it were a favorite bone. A short while later a building came into view.

"I don't believe it!" Garfield exclaimed, twisting Odie's head to get a better look. "It's Santa's workshop! Nimgal wasn't lost at all. He came back to the workshop. And he obviously knew a shortcut that he didn't show us! But why?"

Garfield and Odie followed the footprints to a large stable. Taking the flashlight from Odie, Garfield peeked into the open door. He was stunned by the sight of Nimgal loading a sack full of toys onto Santa's sleigh. In front of the sleigh, Santa's reindeer were fully harnessed, ready for flight.

"You going somewhere, Nimgal?" Garfield asked. "And, by the way, thanks for leaving us stranded out there. It was lovely. I'll have to do it again. Maybe when the next Ice Age comes!"

"Out of my way!" Nimgal shouted. "How did you find your way back? You were supposed to get lost . . . literally! I thought I'd leave you stranded in that cave to get you out of my hair. But it doesn't matter, because I'm taking Santa's sleigh. I'm doing the Christmas flight this year!"

"Where's Santa?" Garfield demanded, moving closer to Nimgal. "From everything I've read, he likes to do this sort of thing by himself!"

"Why should he get all the glory every year, while I play second fiddle, working my beard off?" Nimgal shouted as he loaded a few more presents onto the sleigh. "I want my turn at the big time. And this year I'm taking it. Oh, don't worry. I would never hurt the big guy. He's okay."

Garfield stepped closer to the elf, trying to figure out some way to stop him. "So what did you do, send him to Florida for the winter?"

"I tricked Santa into entering a sub-sub-subbasement storage room in the workshop," Nimgal explained as he tightened the straps on the reindeer.

"Then I slammed the door shut. I was about to padlock it from the outside when I realized that that meddling elf Alfip had followed me down to the storage room. So I locked him in there, too."

"Then you told everyone that Alfip had

kidnapped Santa," Garfield said, filling in the missing pieces of the story. "And when Wumbly brought us here to help, you had to figure out some way to get rid of us."

"Bingo, Sherlock," Nimgal snarled, lifting his right foot onto the sleigh's step, preparing to climb aboard. "Now get out of my way!"

Garfield noticed a golden key dangling from Nimgal's belt. *I wonder*, he thought. "Odie!" he shouted, pointing to the key. "Let's play your favorite game. Fetch! Bring me that golden bone!"

Odie charged at Nimgal, who scrambled up onto the sleigh. Odie followed close at his heels. Nimgal leaped off the front of the sleigh onto a reindeer's back. Odie stayed right with him.

Nimgal and Odie jumped from reindeer to reindeer, like checkers on a checkerboard. The elf slid off, ducked through a reindeer's legs, and started toward the back of the sleigh.

Odie changed direction, bounded from a reindeer, and landed beside Nimgal. He snatched the key with his mouth, then turned to bring the golden "bone" back to Garfield.

"Hey!" shouted Nimgal. "Bring that back!"

"Fat chance," Garfield said as Odie trotted up beside him. Garfield took the key from Odie's mouth, replacing it with the flashlight. "If there's one thing Odie knows—and come to think of it, there is only

one thing—it's how to play fetch. Nice work, Odie. Now let's go free Santa!"

Nimgal climbed back onto the sleigh. "It doesn't matter," he said, grabbing the reins. "By the time you get him free, I'll be long gone with these toys, games, and that huge box of candy canes!"

The elf spun around, realizing that he had forgotten something. "Now where are those candy canes?" he muttered, rummaging through the giant sack. "I can't visit the children of the world on Christmas Eve without candy canes!"

Looking up, Garfield spotted an enormous box of candy canes on a shelf near the front door to the stable. "Wow!" he shouted. At the sight of all that brightly colored sugar, Garfield's mind went blank. He lost track of everything else and leaped up to grab the box.

Garfield's paw caught the edge of the

box, but he couldn't maintain a solid grip. The huge box came tumbling down, leaving him buried under a mountain of red-and-white sticks.

"I've got your presents!" he said excitedly.

One candy cane struck a nearby lever. The door to the stable began to lower, like a mechanical garage door. "Come on, Odie, that's our cue to get out of here," Garfield shouted, stuffing candy canes into his pockets.

As Garfield and Odie dashed for the door, Nimgal tightened his grip on the reins. "On Dasher! On Dancer! On Prancer! On Vixen!" he shouted.

The reindeer took a step forward, then stopped as the door slid down before them.

"No!" Nimgal cried, leaping from the sleigh. "I've got to get that door open!"

Garfield and Odie slipped under the door, which was now only inches from the ground. Just before the door closed, Garfield reached back in and grabbed another fistful of candy canes. Spotting a padlock on the outside of the stable door, Garfield locked Nimgal in.

“Let me out!” Nimgal screamed, banging on the door. “The children need their gifts.”

“And *Santa* will deliver them,” Garfield replied. Then he turned and ran toward the workshop with Odie at his side.

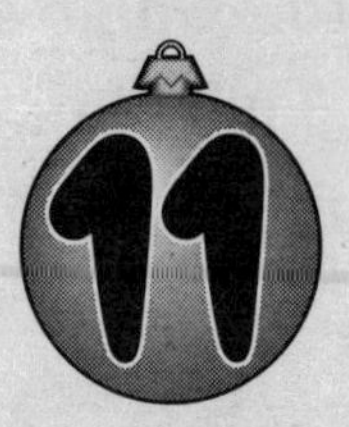

Garfield and Odie burst into Santa's workshop.

Wumbly was leading a line of worried elves in a group pace, back and forth across the workshop floor. Everything was ready for Christmas. Everything, that is, except Santa.

"You're back!" Wumbly shouted. "Have you found Santa?"

"Yes," Garfield reported.

Wumbly looked behind Garfield's back. He saw only Odie gripping the flashlight firmly in his teeth.

“Well, where is he?” Wumbly asked. “It’s time for him to leave!”

“He’s right under your feet,” Garfield replied. “No time to explain. Can you lead me to the sub-sub-subbasement?”

Wumbly’s eyes opened wide. “Follow me,” he said.

Garfield followed Wumbly down a circular stairway. The stairs wound around and around and seemed to go down forever.

“I think someone should give Santa an elevator for Christmas,” Garfield moaned, growing dizzy as he descended into the workshop’s basements.

At last they reached the bottom of the stairs, where they came to a padlocked door. Garfield shoved the golden key into the lock. It popped open and the door swung inward. In a dank, cobweb-covered room filled with toy parts, sleigh harnesses, and candy molds sat Santa and an elf.

“Santa! Alfip!” Wumbly shouted. “Are you all right?”

“Wumbly!” Santa cried, struggling to his feet. “You’ve come to rescue us! *AH-CHOO!*” Santa let out an enormous sneeze.

“Not me, Santa,” Wumbly said, offering him a green-and-red polka-dotted hanky. “It was Garfield and Odie who rescued you.”

"Thank you," Santa said, breaking into a coughing fit that ended with another huge sneeze. "We're tired and hungry. And I seem to have picked up a terrible cold from this damp place."

"Where is Nimgal?" demanded Alfip. "That . . . that . . . ooh, he makes me so mad! The nerve of locking Santa up. I almost stopped him, too, but then he shoved me in here and locked the door!"

"Yes," Santa said, sneezing again.

"Where is Nimgal?"

"We've got him locked in the stable," Garfield explained. "He tried to take your sleigh and do your job this year."

"Hmm," Santa said, blowing his nose. "I feel awful. I really don't think that I'm up to the task of delivering all those presents tonight. I need someone to take my place, but it certainly won't be Nimgal!"

Santa turned to Garfield. "You seem to be the strong and brave type, coming all this way to rescue me," he said, placing a hand on Garfield's shoulder. "Would you fill in for me tonight? *AH-CHOO!*"

Garfield looked over his shoulder. "I'm sorry. We're you talking to me? I heard the words *brave* and *strong*, so I figured you must be talking to someone else."

"Please, Garfield," Santa said. "I need you to make this journey."

"I don't know," Garfield said. "Traveling from the living room to the kitchen is an exhausting journey for me. You want me to go all the way around the world?"

"You know," Santa began, "boys and girls all over the world leave out milk and cookies for me. You'll be able to eat a plateful of cookies at each of the millions of stops you make. One year, someone in Italy even left me an entire lasagna!"

Garfield headed for the door. "Let's go," he said. "Wouldn't want that lasagna to get cold!"

"The only problem is," Santa continued, "the weather forecasts are predicting big snowstorms in many places around the world tonight. My reindeer will have a tough time finding their way as they fly."

Garfield glanced down at Odie, who still had Nimgal's flashlight clutched in his slobbering mouth. Its bright beam lit up the dark storage room.

"Odie, who is not too bright, won't you guide the sleigh tonight?" Garfield asked.

Odie nodded his agreement.

"Thank you both," Santa said. Then he looked up at the long, winding stairway and sighed. "I think next year I'll put in an elevator!"

After climbing back up all those stairs, Garfield, Odie, Santa, Wumbly, and Alfip hurried to the stable. Using the golden key to open the padlock, Santa flung open the door. He found Nimgal slumped against the sleigh with his chin in his hands.

"Santa!" Nimgal cried, jumping to his feet. "I'm so sorry. I did such a foolish thing. Will you ever forgive me?"

"Of course I forgive you—*AH-CHOO!*" Santa said. "However, I have a little task for you. To make up for your foolishness, you will please clean up that horrible, damp storage room. Then install a dehumidifier and a small fridge in the room, just in case anyone else ever gets locked in—accidentally!"

"And when you're done with that," Garfield added, "there's a nice yeti who lives in that cave on the top of the mountain. I'm sure he'd appreciate knowing that Santa is okay."

"I'll get right on it, Santa," Nimgal said humbly. "And Garfield, Odie, I'm sorry for all the trouble I caused. As soon as I'm done cleaning up the storage room, I'll go back and tell the yeti what happened." Then Nimgal headed for the workshop.

Santa helped Garfield up onto the sleigh, then handed him his long list of stops. He strapped Odie into the lead harness in front of the reindeer. The flashlight still shone brightly.

"How can I possibly make all these stops in one night?" Garfield asked, looking over the list.

"Ah," said Santa, smiling. "That's the magic of Christmas!" Then he unleashed another monstrous sneeze.

With Odie lighting the way, the reindeer trotted from the stable, then lifted into the air. The sleigh rose higher and higher into the night sky with Garfield at the reins, a candy cane sticking out of his mouth, and Santa's big sack of gifts behind him.

As the sleigh disappeared from view, Santa heard Garfield say:

"I heard him exclaim, 'ere he drove out of sight, 'Merry Christmas to all, can we stop for a bite?'"

## Epilogue

Christmas morning dawned bright and clear. The snow had stopped falling outside Jon's house. Late on Christmas Eve, Jon finally had dozed off on the couch, waiting for his pets to return.

The front door swung open and in trudged Garfield and Odie, looking exhausted.

"Merry Christmas!" Jon exclaimed, leaping from the couch. "I was worried sick about you two. I'm so glad you found a way to get home."

"If you only knew," Garfield mumbled. He and Odie had completed their journey around the world on time, despite eating Christmas cookies on every continent. Returning to the North Pole in the early morning, they had been transported home by the elves' magic.

Jon raced over to the Christmas tree.

"A nap until New Year's Eve would be the best present for me," said Garfield.

Jon handed Garfield a rectangular box. "For you, Garfield!" he said. "Merry Christmas!"

Garfield lifted the lid off the box to reveal a toy bathtub filled with lasagna. "Time for a bath!" he said, his eyes lighting up.

"And this is for you, Odie," Jon said. He handed Odie a giant candy cane, almost as big as the fake one Odie had licked in Santa's workshop. Odie happily licked the huge candy cane, turning his tongue red.

"One more surprise!" Jon said, dashing into the kitchen. He returned a few seconds later with an enormous plate full of Christmas cookies. "Merry Christmas to both of you!"

Garfield pulled his nose out of the lasagna and stared at the mountain of cookies. After all the Christmas cookies he had just eaten on his journey around the world, he didn't know how he could possibly eat another one. Yet he knew that somehow he would find a way.

## About Garfield's Creator

**Jim Davis** was born in Marion, Indiana, and was promptly dropped on his head—which could explain his lifelong desire to be a cartoonist. Jim still lives in the Hoosier state, preferring the quiet joys of country life, where a man can walk his pig in peace.

## About the Author

**Michael Teitelbaum** was born in Brooklyn, New York, at a very early age. As a child he loved cartoons, baseball, and the Marx Brothers. As a grown-up he loves cartoons, baseball, and the Marx Brothers, and is lucky enough to have spent more than twenty years writing books based on cartoons, baseball, and humor. Michael and his wife, Sheleigah, split their time between New York City and their farmhouse in upstate New York.

## About the Illustrator

**Mike Fentz** flunked flute-a-phone lessons in the fourth grade. Fifth grade gave rise to a new career—doodling cartoons in his textbooks. To this day, he's still doodling cartoons in books. Mike lives in Muncie, Indiana, with his wife, Anne, his two daughters, Jessica and Rachel, a cat, and a slightly used guinea pig.